words breathe in silence

Anindita Bose

Ukiyoto Publishing

Dedication

This book is dedicated to myself and my brother.

In the story of our lives, we started walking on the parallel roads, and I believe that one day we will walk together again in our garden, like we did when I was seven and he was five and a half years old…

and

I would like to thank Poet Novelist, Hon. D. Litt. Bob DCosta, without him this journey of 'words breathe in silence' with 'Ukiyoto Publishing' would not have begun…

Introduction:

Short stories as a genre of literature have appealed to me since my formative years of reading. I have been fascinated by the classic short stories of Guy De Maupassant, O Henry, D.H. Lawrence, James Joyce, Anton Chekov, and many more. In the domain of Indian Writing in English, the short stories of Kamala Das in her book 'The Kept Woman and Other Stories' have touched me immensely as a woman and as a writer and I have kept going back to them to understand the multilayered nuances of the characters. In the tradition of Bengali literature, most of us have also explored the works of Rabindranath Tagore and his magnum opus collection of stories 'Galpaguchchho', while marvelling at the storytelling, characterization and the messages that each story unfolds in the collection. While thinking of the famous quote by Haruki Murakami on short story writing: "Short stories are like guideposts to my heart...", the amalgamation of the east and west in my consciousness during the act of reading short fiction has helped me internalise and absorb the essence of the emotional journeys of the fictional characters in unique, incredible ways.

When Anindita Bose, a good friend and a fellow poet and storyteller shared with me her manuscript of short stories titled **words breathe in silence** to read and provide my personal critique on, this quote of Murakami became the springboard to my emotional understanding of each of the stories in the collection, as I was trying to grasp the essence of the symbolism of the characters, their narratives and the underlying meaning and essence of the narratives.

I have previously read a substantial body of Anindita's poetry in her recently published collection **illuminate darkness – the fireflies** and her memoir titled **Motherhood and I** which is part of the anthology of memoirs and personal essays, 'The Body of Memories' that I was privileged to edit, apart from her other published pieces online, and I have noticed how the poetic voice of hers have evolved in her verse and also in her prose in course of time, but in **words breathe in silence**, I have been delighted to witness her growth as a storyteller in terms of development of plot and narrative style, marrying prose with the lyricism of poetry.

Contemporary storytelling in the hands of today's Indian writers writing in the English language has evolved considerably, reflecting the ethos of our postmodern world. We can say in all fairness that some new age writers and storytellers have come a long way, depicting some of the richness of classic literary fiction through symbolism, lyricism in their storytelling, while also breathing new life to their stories by infusing their modernist sensibilities into the stories. After reading Anindita's stories in the collection, I can strongly contend that she is one of those new age writers with a unique voice, and a penchant for freshness in her richly descriptive and meaningful fictional tales. The themes of her stories in the collection range from the very surreal, symbolic to the strife-ridden realities of marriage, relationships and interpersonal equations in modern Indian settings, and through the unfolding of each tale, she presents a complex, intriguing mosaic of the idiosyncrasies and quirks, sweetness and bitterness of the humane realities around us.

To quote a few significant opening lines from one of her stories titled 'Drug Store':

"Love is neither blind nor selfish. It is a drug that pulls one out of a comfort zone and puts one in a new state. The heart pumps faster the moment the syringe enters this drug into the cells of a body that is unaware of the emotion, and then begins a story of disruption."

The theme of the story here, like a few other stories penned by the writer, is that of contemporary urban relationship between man and woman and the underlying strife in their journey. However, what is remarkable to my understanding is her use of language and imagery that breathes in a unique postmodern style and adds to the very ethos of her literary, cultural understanding.

As a collection of modern short stories, I can relate to this book very much for the insights and the metaphorical realities that the writer weaves in her narratives. I wish her a wide readership for the book.

Lopamudra Banerjee

Acclaimed Author, Poet, Translator, Editor
Faculty of Writing, University of North Texas, Texas Christian University, USA

After reading Anindita Bose's book – 'words breathe in silence' I have a few lines to express my thoughts about her stories.

"I noticed in the society how the women were given chances to bloom only to be crushed repeatedly," writes Anindita Bose in one of these stories in which she combines attention to daily life with another dimension that seems to come from a soul who is many years older than she is, a young woman who has been raised in Kolkata and listens to the secret vibration emanating from things and events, like a trail of sounds which, however, leads everything back into that original love from which we come.

Franca Mancinelli
(Translated by John Taylor)

Franca Mancinelli (Fano, Italy, 1981), is widely considered to be one of the most compelling voices in Italian poetry. She is the author of four books of poetry: *Mala kruna* (2007), *Pasta madre* [*Mother Dough*] 2013, *Libretto di transito* [*The Little Book of Passage*] 2018, *Tutti gli occhi che ho aperto* [*All the Eyes that I have Opened*] 2020. Her writing has been translated into several foreign languages and published in journals and anthologies. In John Taylor's English translations have appeared in the United States by The Bitter Oleander Press (Fayetteville, New York), *The Little Book of Passage* (2018), *At an Hour's Sleep from Here: Poems* (2007-2019), and *The Butterfly Cemetery: Selected Prose (2008-2021)*.

Contents

Sometimes You Are Your Own Ship ...

in search of you sometimes I have lost myself,
but you never wished to walk my way ...

Mosquitoes

Written in Ooty

"I want to see a mosquito!" The voice of a little girl brought me back to the park, in which I was walking aimlessly. Why a mosquito, was the first thought and then an irritation. I was busy. My life needed some discussions and decisions. And in such a significant moment a voice wanted to see a mosquito. Wait a minute, wasn't this a cold place?

"There are no mosquitoes here!" I looked at the tiny girl. Why do they even get permission to leave their homes? It was around six in the evening; she must be home doing some homework. "Are you alone?"

"No, my governess has gone to find a mosquito," she said excitedly.

"There are no mosqui…," oh let it be, she was a little girl after all. I started walking away but she came running and held my right hand.

"So do you think they all died? Or flew away?" She asked.

"Listen, I have better things to do…" but the way her eyes examined me I had to laugh. "Okay, they are in the plains; they do not like the hill station."

"Then why did my governess go to find them?" She asked. Now how would I know that? I looked around. There was no one. I took her to a bench nearby and we both sat silently for a few seconds before she broke the silence. "I never liked her anyway…"

Her name was Anshu and she was seven years old. Every evening she came to play in that park. She was filling me up with information. I wished that she vanished so that I could think in solace, but the world cannot be kind. And she demanded that I listen to her, and told me stories that could send an adult to the fairy-tale world, which he might have deliberately left behind. I wanted some space from my life and came to that park for a silent walk. Anshu's words took me to another dimension in which I could see several images of my own.

I closed my eyes and opened them again to check. But I saw the same thing. A child-me, a teenage-me, in twenties-me, in thirties-me... I looked at Anshu and she was still that little girl of seven, sitting and blabbering. For a while I was sure that I was very stressed; and the images were definitely in my mind.

I visited that place since there were certain issues on my mind. Recently I had left my job to be with my husband and that decision had changed my entire life. For some days I felt that my husband was not listening to me and perhaps I was taken for granted. Our marriage was five years old and we did not plan a child. We shifted to Rajgarh from Calcutta a year back and after four months I left my job. He had nothing to say and days were passing by like the clouds on rainy days - slowly and swiftly. And then one day the thoughts crawled into my mind, *what if he was seeing another woman?*

There have been changes in our lifestyles. I could barely make any new friends in that new town. He was busy with his new promoted position. I was alone most of the days, doing household work or trimming the garden. He was busy with his work, and almost each day he was tired and preferred sleeping early in the nights. In the initial four months I worked from home. After a few days I tried exploring the place. I found a few things different from Calcutta but as the months passed everything became familiar. There was nothing new anymore. Each corner of that place reminded me of my hometown, and sometimes I could find old memories etched in the walls and trees. Even though Rajganj was a place I had never visited before, I started believing that all places in this world are similar after a few months. The streets, the houses, the walls, the sky, the birds, the parks, the people... but it is odd that we change. We get bored of the similitude.

Our relationship has been special, we never believed in breaking the patterns, rather we liked being quiet and together. Yet after being in Rajganj for a few months I wondered why we talked less or why we never went out on Sundays. There was no plan of marriage when he had met for the first time. But our families wanted us to decide the wedding date, and it was my husband who declared his wish to marry within a month. After that, each Sunday he took me out for shopping and then dinner. After four Sundays we had tied the knot. Everything was planned well, yet something seemed out of order.

I was watching my other selves playing with each other. They were cheering and playing with a red ball. I was quite confused at that sight, and something inside me told me that I was dreaming. It was possible since before walking towards the park, I had taken a sleeping pill because I wanted to sleep as soon as I reached back home.

But then the child-me came and sat beside me!

I looked at her intensely. She smiled and said, "Do you know me?"

"Well, I think so," nothing made sense to me.

The child-me laughed and said, "This is what you always did. Changed the present and kept thinking about those things that made no sense…"

"What do you mean?" I could not believe she said that. But before I could give her a piece of my mind the teenage-me came and shoved her away. She looked at me and asked, "Do you still believe her?"

"What do you mean? She looks like my…"

"Yes, maybe but she is definitely not you! Look at me, I am more of you. You told me all your secrets and lived more around me…"

I looked at her; she was wearing one of those jackets that I loved the most once. She had a tattoo in the fingers of her left hand and was wearing my favourite earrings. "If you believe so," I said with a shrug.

"You are mistaken. I do not think so. It is you who thinks that you resemble me even now!"

How could these non-existent entities speak like that? I asked her to leave because there was no need for such arrogance in my life; I needed peace. But as I wished, she got up, waved to the twenties-me and left. The woman in her twenties came and sat next to me. I looked at Anshu and she was still talking. What has happened to that little girl? Can she not see the others who were visiting me?

The twenties-me laughed, "Why are you even bothered? You hardly care!"

"What do you mean?" I looked at her. That same t-shirt! One of my aunts had bought it for me from Delhi when I was twenty-three years old.

"Yes, I knew you would stare, the same one. That woman is dead now so stop thinking about her." She said in a cold voice.

"She was my aunt!"

"So? She was the one who said you could leave home and be in a living relationship. And you did!"

"What is your problem? I loved that man and I wanted to be with him…" I could not imagine that I was talking about a past relationship so openly in a park.

"Oh, and that got you into all that trouble." She got up with rage and walked away.

"Stop!" I wanted to converse more with her. But the thirties-me was already staring at me and laughing.

"Why are you laughing?" I hated her.

"She would never listen to you; did you listen to her?" At that moment I wished that image of mine disappeared forever.

"I would never leave you alone. At least for another five years I will keep coming to you."

"Why?"

"You need me. You have already wasted many years."

I could not understand her accusations. I stared blankly at her.

"Look, what else do you expect from life? Whatever you had wanted you have received." She said and took out a cigarette. The smoke circled in the air. I looked at Anshu and she was still lost in her world.

"I don't understand," I said.

"You were thirty-one when you married Jatin and even after that you did not stop meeting Akash. Jatin still doesn't know about your one-month live-in relationship with Akash! Yet after that final managerial promotion you received, you even went for a solo trip with him."

"No. I did not do any such things!" I had once imagined that I would go on a trip with Akash, when there was an argument with Jatin, and when my husband had made it clear that he would not sleep in the same room. But I was sure that I had never broken the vows of our marriage to go on a trip with my lover.

"Of course, it was not you. But me!" She laughed.

I wanted to break free. I tried to stand up, but my feet were stuck into the roots of that tree under which Anshu and I were sitting. I looked at the little girl; her feet were also taken by those roots. I looked at the thirties-me, but she had walked far away from us. And all of a sudden, the clouds rolled in and we heard the thunder. It was already dark and it could rain anytime. I looked around and realised that the park was looking like a green mountain. I heard Anshu. She was struggling to say something. I touched her shoulders but she did not notice or perhaps ignored me. I knew she was scared as much as I was.

The place was rapidly transforming. I heard Anshu again, "Governess… governess… where are you? I want to see a mosquito…" There was no one, but us. I tried to open my eyes; I thought it was a dream. I had seen such dreams before. But I was wide awake. I tried telling Anshu that I was there and I would take care of everything, like I always do. Yet no words came out of my mouth. In a fraction of seconds, we could hear the thunder again and I could hear the rain coming. Yes, the rain! The water drops will change our lives. We will have new days again. We waited. Anshu was scared. I waited eagerly, yet no rain came. But we heard wings flapping and then we saw hundreds of mosquitoes coming towards us.

"Stop it!" I screamed. "Stop them! They will bite."

Someone pushed a painful injection into my left arm. I heard Anshu scream too; I tried looking at her but I could not. I was already drowsy and the green mountain was turning into a dark abyss. The roots were holding me tightly and the clouds silently rolled by. The rain did not come. I wanted to sleep. It was time. And there were no reasons why I would stay awake. I heard laughter. Somehow, I managed to look up and saw my other selves laughing at me. I gave up, I could not do anything. The injected medicine was more powerful, and my drowsy eyes slowly closed.

"Mr. Jatin Roy? It's not time yet! The meeting time is at four in the evening." Dr. Mallika Ghosh came and stood beside Radhika Roy's husband. She was on the rounds to check her patients, and had just injected Radhika with Invega Trinza.

"I know Dr. Ghosh. How is she doing?" Mr. Roy looked lost, but his eyes were fixed on the closed door of the patient's cabin.

"Well, she found a little girl this time, a seven years old Anshu."

"Oh, I see. Good. But she never finds me…," Jatin sounded quite serious.

"Mr. Roy, when are you getting married?" Dr. Ghosh asked, looking into Jatin's eyes.

"Next month." He said in an uncomfortable cold voice. "Anyways, can I meet her?" He asked while killing a mosquito that flew from nowhere and sat on his forehead.

"Yes. She is sleeping. You can see her now. But if you want to talk then you have to wait till four in the evening." Dr. Ghosh smiled sympathetically at him.

"It would be better if I could see her now." Jatin said without thinking much.

Dr. Ghosh nodded and took him to room number twenty-five. "I wonder where that mosquito came from in this cold place!" She said before leaving the husband alone in the cabin to see his wife.

death became a tragedy
only when I crossed paths with
those, who could breathe words
into my ears ...

Distant Mist

Written in Kolkata

The cat stopped moving. I am not sure when she stopped moving but at that moment in time she was not moving. I kept nudging her still body but she did not stir from her silent sleep. I touched her soft yellow stained coloured chest, looking for a heartbeat. Nothing. I waited patiently for the sudden 'meow' and demands for petting while covering my dress in yellow sticky hair; silly cat hair that defied washing and clinging on to my apparel in silent rebellious contempt to water. The cat had died.

I called her Autumn since she reminded me of the colours of fall from the Instagram posts my cousin had once posted for the season. Such vivid brownish yellow, such soft delicate eyes and whiskers! Did she really die? The reality of the situation throbbed in my mind with the question. Maybe she died because she was cold. The winters of Kolkata have gone so cold lately. Maybe poor, warm weather loving Autumn could not stand this weather. Maybe I should have wrapped her in my blanket to keep her warm and safe. My stomach felt sick, my hands numb, I wanted to curl up next to her and just lie there with her. I nudged her again before leaving her alone in the living room.

"NEAL! NEAL!" I called out to my brother knowing he would ignore my calls. We have to make space in our garden for Autumn. I kept calling and finally he shouted back from his room "WHAT IS IT?" I could hear the bass of his second-hand speakers blasting from the closed door. Our parents were not home and the cigarette stench was seeping through the cracks as he and his friends were enjoying the time of freedom from parental supervision. He hated cats, he hated the idea of cats, and he hated my love for the cats. He hated cats breaking the boundaries of walls, encroaching his space and demanding attention.

My eyes threatened to spill the tears it had been holding back as I shouted back behind the door "I need your help" please, I added silently. I needed to finish the last rituals for Autumn's death.

After waiting for ten more minutes, I decided to break into his room. At that moment Neal's friend Kiren came and asked what help I needed. I looked at her for five seconds and then said, "My cat Autumn needs a grave."

Her jaw dropped and she was silent for some time, then nodded. We went to the sitting room. Autumn was lying on the white carpet where I had left her. For a second I hoped that she would jump into life and come to my feet. Cats have a way with their owners, they always move around their feet and make their presence felt. Nothing happened. The setting was like a movie scene: a silent room, one open window, a light breeze coming in and the curtains moving, three empty sofas, furniture, and a white carpet with a dead cat. Kiren looked surprised, so was me since I found myself smiling, lost in my subconscious thoughts. Autumn was fine that morning and she was a young cat. However, I stopped thinking and looked at Kiren, who was as lost in thoughts as I was seconds before.

"Shall we?" I asked.

"Yes!" She sounded distant.

We went to the garden. Took a spade and made a nice grave. I brought Autumn in a cardboard box. Took her out and put her in that hole in which she shall lie forever. How soft she was in my hands; I felt like squeezing her. I wondered how it would be to try and crush her, to squeeze her really hard. Will she meow back?

"Stop!" Kiren almost screamed in my ears. Oh, I was actually squeezing Autumn. I immediately put her in that grave we had made and we covered it with mud. Then I brought a rose plant from one of the pots and planted it on top of Autumn's grave. Kiren looked inquisitively.

"She loved roses!" I tried to explain. She looked even more puzzled. "I mean she had destroyed most of the rose plants, so I thought she must have liked to play with roses," I explained in a calm voice. She nodded and left me in the garden alone with my dead cat's grave. I had always felt that women have a special liking for cats, but when

Kiren left without shedding any tears, I realised perhaps it was my imagination. I must have been two years old when my father brought a kitten home. And since then, my cats were always replaced as each of them passed away. But Autumn, my ninth cat, came to our home by herself one afternoon after Misty died under a neighbour's car in front of our house two years ago.

Autumn was a stray kitten and my mother had said that I cannot keep her. It was such a struggle that I had gone through to keep that little kitten! There was a kind of attraction that I had felt for her; a connection that I could never explain to my parents.

I focused on the present situation.

The problem was my intuition, which had told me two years back that Autumn would be my last cat if she died suddenly. It was a Sunday morning; I woke up as usual and looked for my new kitten. She was tiny and beautiful. I wanted to feed her myself, and so I looked for her everywhere.

"Papa, have you seen Autumn?" I asked my father who was sitting on the balcony, reading the newspaper.

"Strange kitten Maya. How did you find her?"

"Why Papa? You know she came from nowhere…"

"Yes, yes. Look in the garden beneath the banyan tree."

I ran into the garden and saw Autumn sitting there. I wondered if cats could meditate, since her posture looked like she was doing that. I was young and all I wanted was fun moments in life. I went and picked Autumn up, cuddled her and fed her milk. But suddenly as I was walking back to the house, something happened. It was like a hallucination or a déjà vu; I never understood. I saw Autumn in that garden, sitting under that banyan tree and looking at me and a voice from far away saying, be careful and take care of her because if she died then you will never have a cat again. I turned and looked back but there was nothing. It was perhaps my imagination, I had thought. A passionate reader of books may develop a stream of consciousness occasionally.

After two-and-a half years she died just like that. I was now sure that

I would never have a cat again. I was reflecting on this when I heard laughter behind me. I turned. It was Neal.

"Why are you laughing?" I asked in a sad voice.

"Why not? Look, your cat is dead! Didn't I tell you to keep her locked…?"

"What? What did you do NEAL?" Suddenly fear and anger gripped me and my knees shivered.

"Nothing."

"Liar!"

"Shut up. I did not do anything."

My mind raced. Autumn was a life in a cat's body. Any life form is significant on this earth and if she was murdered then I was responsible too, since I was her guardian. I focused on Neal's body language. Was it possible? Oh, I could never again have a pet in my life since I was guilty of not being able to take care of my own cat. But could my seventeen-year-old brother be that brutal? Was it at all making any sense…?

"Okay fine. I did not kill Autumn, you did." He laughed cruelly.

"I did? What do you mean Neal?"

"I gave her animal tranquillizers with milk. And you buried her under that tree, silly girl." "Impossible, your cruel heart," I said, my voice quivered with emotions and fear.

"A little extra dose and that must have slowed her heartbeats. Did you look for her heartbeats properly? Look, I am sorry, but she always pissed in my room and I hated that. I just wanted to teach her and you a lesson." He said this in his most casual voice, shrugged his broad shoulders and walked towards the house. I stood there like a stone. Before entering the house, he looked back and said, "She was only a cat. It's okay, you can forgive yourself!"

I knew I would not forgive either myself or Neal. On that day I had taken the spade again to bring Autumn out but a fear gripped me and I could not dare to think how a half dead cat might look in the grave. I became a coward at that moment and I could never forgive myself for that. I looked one last time at the banyan tree, beneath which Autumn was buried, perhaps gasping for air or scratching the mud with her tiny claws…struggling to live or die.

I ran to my room and closed the door behind me.

chances lost are not opportunities gone,
they are just passing moments to remind us
that life has different pages ...

The Chance Before The Last

Written in Mumbai

It is Mumbai after all, a city of dreams and desires that brings people from all parts of India to live their wishful lives. From aspiring actors, filmmakers, to students with hopes of jobs, and villagers in search of work, all travel to the city of Mumbai if they can dare to. What they do there or how they spend their days in that city are curiosities that cannot be known unless people visit the city and observe for some days. But who has time for such studies when India is actually reaching closer to the first world countries' philosophy of living a fast life and a life of solitude.

Today every Indian wishes to achieve success in a short period of time, and the way of life itself has become competitive and irrational at times. A country needs to change in the modern time, and each generation needs to be different and better. Mumbai is that symbol city of India which holds opportunities for those who can break the barriers of traditional family rules and reach that soil along the Arabian Sea.

Francis reached Mumbai on a different note. He had thought and accepted the fact that this was his last chance to do something in life. Why he concluded this about his life, will take us to flashback. Perhaps like any young boy he had not taken life seriously before and then one day fate must have come in the form of some dark moment in his life and jolted his existence. And the young Francis' life demanded his attention immediately. He discussed with his family and took up a competitive course in Mumbai and reached the city in October 2018.

But there was a twist in this story - the difference of cultures and tradition. Francis was from South India, the part of India that did not let their children forget the traditions. And therefore, he did not break any barriers to reach the city. He took consent from his family, enrolled himself for a course, packed his bags and stepped into that city. Initially he had doubts, and he kept saying to himself that this was his last chance to do something. He started his classes, took a rented room in a hostel and focused on his studies. It was a very rigorous course that required him to concentrate and give his full time. Francis was determined to do everything that was required to prove himself to his family.

The days passed. Francis did quite well in his course and achieved appreciation from his professors and batch mates. His scores were good, and deep within his heart he started believing that perhaps his family would know that he was capable of achieving better things in life. But then came his birthday. It could have been a simple day like the other days if Francis had not gone to the Juhu beach that night. He went to have a free walk along the sea and feel the cool breeze. The place where his home was had nature in abundance. It was Ooty, a serene hill station in Tamil Nadu and far away from the hustle-bustle of the city. Even though he had been to Bangalore and Hyderabad before, Mumbai was absolutely a different space. It was a conglomerate of different people with distinct cultures and values. And no one judged any actions in that city of Bollywood.

Francis had already realised the truth about the city and while he was walking on that beach which apparently was not clean but had a sense of peace, he thought - where am I going to go from here? He looked up at the dark sky; there were no stars but a kind of blankness that gave a chance to fill it up with images of one's own imagination. He had already learned in life how to be with himself. In the company of relatives or distant friends usually he kept quiet and listened more. Mumbai cannot change him. He smiled when he remembered what some neighbours had discussed before he had come to the city – that place would change him; and how worried his parents had been about those words. But Francis knew that nothing can ever change his innate self. He always believed that goodness was not a choice but a quality inherited from the family that one belonged to.

But what happened on his birthday night?

He was lost in his thoughts about life, and his last chance in life when he noticed the man. He saw a bubble seller who could blow the most beautiful bubbles that he had ever seen. He kept staring for five minutes and then bought one. He had never before blown bubbles in public and it seemed quite naïve to him. But that night he wanted to do it and he did. All shapes of bubbles flew around him and above the sea. The sea played with the waves along his feet and he was lost in a different world. And then it happened. Suddenly he felt that someone was walking towards him. He looked around but did not notice anyone worth seeing. He focused on his bubbles and checked the time once. It was fine to reach the hostel late, and it was his birthday. But still he wanted to be conscious about the time. Again, he felt that someone was walking towards him. His intuition was strong like most people's sixth sense who belonged to the Scorpio zodiac. Again, he looked sharply to his left where a police patrolling car was parked. And then he saw a little girl walking towards him; there was some abnormality in her gait. But she kept walking straight towards him and came very close; her eyes were fixed on him. But later he realised that her eyes were actually fixed on the pink bubble bottle that was in his hands. He smiled. But he decided not to look at her. She was a simple slum girl who loitered around the Juhu beach like many other slum dwellers did at night. The beaches in Mumbai were places for their entertainment and the free breeze was their relief from the warm climate.

The little girl came to him and spread out her palm. He tried to ignore her, but could not since she was too straightforward in her demand. He took out a five-rupee coin and gave it to her but she did not take it. It was clear that she wanted the bubble bottle. Francis could have walked away; instead, he looked at the sea in front of them and gave that bottle to her. The girl smiled sheepishly and walked away to the direction from where she had come. He tried to see if anyone was with her or not, but there was no one. He walked and sat on the sea beach, now with nothing to do he thought it was better to go back. The next day was Monday and a busy day. But just as he was about to get up a man came and sat beside him.

"I saw what you did. Good!" The man said.

"Just like that," Francis said.

"I come here almost every day. I never see people, especially young boys like you doing that." The man smiled.

"Well…"

"Where are you from?"

"Tamil Nadu."

"I see. what are you doing here?"

Francis wanted to tell, working on my last chance. Instead, he said, "Doing a course."

"My name is Mohanraj. I am a journalist. This city has once given me the chance before the last." The man said and winked at Francis.

"The chance before the last? What does that mean?" Francis was curious.

"Well, there is nothing called a last chance in life. Quite a human made concept. But when I came to Mumbai, I thought I could do nothing with my life." He looked at Francis. "And now I am quite a successful journalist. Yes, we need to work hard but this city has a charm." Francis must have looked surprised since the man put a hand on his shoulders and said, "I have no idea why I am saying this to you but when I saw what you did, something inside me told that I must talk to you."

The young man smiled. He knew life could play strange games at times and this could be one of them. But he liked Mohanraj for some reasons and listened to him carefully, while the breeze played with the waves near them.

"Look Francis, I don't know why you are here on this beach now. Or why I am here, but the fact is everything has a reason."

Francis nodded. He thought that he understood the purpose of that meeting. But he remained quiet.

"One day you will understand. And this happens to all of us. Life gives us moments to realise certain things. Right now, I don't know why I decided to say these to you. Perhaps my heart is broken and I am missing my home…," Mohanraj looked lost for a second.

"Are you okay?" Francis asked.

"Yes, yes, my boy. Oh, look at the time. I must go." He gave a light hug to Francis and walked away. Francis kept staring at the man. After a few seconds the man turned back and waved goodbye. Francis did the same. The man shouted back, "We may not meet again, since you did not ask for my phone number or social media details. But remember there is nothing called a last chance in life. Each day has a new promise, learn to identify that and live a happy life junior!"

Francis stood in that same spot for the next ten minutes. His phone rang. It was Thomas, his brother. "Happy Birthday once again Francis. Have a great life ahead!"

"Thank you *anna*, I will."

*letting go is not an option, but unless we
let go, we cannot learn how to
hold back the loved ones ...*

Homecoming

Written in Pondicherry

The door was open. The home belonged to a family living in Calcutta for seventy years, and built by a couple who came from the border of Bangladesh at the dawn of Indian freedom. Why the home was built in the first place has an interesting story. One evening, while they were sitting together in their rented house the wife, Ashima told her husband that they must build a home.

"Why? You know we have a family of five brothers, two sisters and I am the earning member. We also have our own children. A house means money..." the husband said in a serious tone.

"No, not a house. A home. We need it for our children. Tell me something, would you enter a big home while passing by it on a random day?" Ashima asked. Her eyes were curious to know what her husband thought.

"Never, if I do not know the owner!" Sometimes he knew that his wife imagined the future and lived far away in time. He believed in her wisdom.

She said after a while, "If we have a home, magnificent and majestic one, even if we do not have enough money to eat good food and I feed our children plants from the garden, isn't it true that people will think twice before entering our home?"

He looked into her eyes. She knew how to convince him, "Yes, they will do that even in the years to come my love. And our house will be a safe place, like a fort."

And now that home was waiting, the door was open. The clouds rolled by, the birds came and went, the sun rose and fell each day. The children have grown, some left and some stayed behind. The photographs of the couple could be seen at various walls of the home and perhaps through them their essence remained.

It was three months that the family came to know about the tumour; not that they were not aware, but no one in the family suffered before. Also, who would worry or research about something that has not affected them personally. Now they know that there are various kinds of tumours and their stages. For the treatment of the loved one they went from one hospital to the other and finally felt helpless when they realised that Calcutta needed a revolution in the arena of hospital management. It was 2018 and perhaps there were places on Earth that had already been kind enough to take care of the patients afflicted by the modern diseases. However, there are different stories in the world and this one was a common one.

The loved one got cured in South India, a place that still believed in wisdom and love. But the journey of any medical care can never be easy. And for days the home remained silent. The travel from Bengal to South was a mammoth task and the middle-class family struggled to get back to the mundane life again. The home witnessed the entry of a crisis, while the family members went through the cycles of life.

Once the home had people, there was laughter and joy, there were fights and accusations, there were dreams and sorrows and in three months the voices turned into whispers. The son of the couple who had built the home, was the father now and he always wanted authority. Everyone must listen to the head of the family no matter what; sometimes the daughter of the family wanted to spread her wings and fly away, but she could not. The son of the family married and gave birth to a girl child, the mother of the family spent her days in her own ways. But the family catastrophe interchanged all roles and altered the entire story.

The loved one, the mother of the family, needed attention and everyone scattered to bring a change soon. Human cells die when they grow old or when their work is done and, in their places, new cells take birth; nature has made humans a phoenix within and without. And when that family needed to solve the complication, their genetic function went through a rebirth and each one transformed in different ways.

The father had always thought that no one would ever leave home. It was after all a home built with care and meant to be always the same.

He took pride in his ancestral creation and how none could build a home like that one. And after three months he realised how life played games. But life and living were not illusions.

We are perhaps those simple cells within our skins that silently keep working, living, dying and continuing the cycle. The father came out of the door each day and waited for them to come back. He stayed alone in the home since his wife was going through the journey of healing.

divorces are like regular break-ups,
and not battles lost forever ...

Maya

Written in Kolkata

'*Could have been a yesterday, but I chose a tomorrow and that is how we reached home together*'

Maya wrote the last line in the letter and put it in a red envelope. The paper had a smell of rose petals. That was one of her wedding gifts to her husband, Robert. The wedding was a week away and they had decided not to meet each other. They wanted to see if they would miss each other or not. Robert told Maya many times how she did not know the meaning of missing a loved one. Maya never fell in love before, but Robert did lose a lover. She laughed and never said a word to him. Instead, she decided to focus on her marriage and post marriage life.

She was marrying late, since she never believed in relationships. She witnessed broken marriages and fights between her parents. So, she wanted to remain single. But meeting Robert somehow changed her choices. Sometimes in life certain moments are inevitable and humans have no control on them. Maya was successful and carefree. She became quite adamant with time. Neither she listened to anyone nor did she care to tell anyone about her views. She kept her focus on her career and travelling since her grandfather passed away. He was dear to her heart.

But Robert was married once, and he told this to Maya after a few days of their informal courtship. Maya could have reacted and even left him but something held her back. Robert was going through his divorce when he met Maya and he did not for once think that he would be in a relationship with a woman who neither belonged to his religion nor his culture. In fact, while going through his divorce trials he was painfully missing his first love Jenny. Robert and Jenny's relationship broke some years before he was emotionally forced to marry a girl from his town by his parents. There were some family issues that put Jenny in a dilemma and she left Robert.

Yet things would have been different if his parents had not decided to intervene and get him married within six months of his break up. Robert was not ready but he saw no hope in his life and kept silent. He smiled on that day, and accepted his fate but he could not balance his dreams and realities. And soon there were quarrels and misunderstandings leading to a divorce. He could have sacrificed his happiness and adjusted with his wife but one day while he was returning home, he felt empty. The thought that he is dying slowly made him uncomfortable and he realised how easily he had started smoking and drinking. That was the moment when he knew that a divorce was the solution.

Maya laughed at this conclusion. She could not accept the reason for the divorce. When she came to know about the story, she was silent for three days. She thought that she must leave and let go of him. But something made her stay, and she still cannot understand what it was. She cried and told herself how unlucky she was that finally when she decided to be in a relationship after all those years of being alone, she met a man who could not manage his affairs. Was it a good idea to be with him? What if he actually makes another mistake and her life would be in a terrible mess? Maya did not know what to do and decided to question him. After three days, she went to meet him. She was about to ask him the questions when he smiled and gave her a yellow rose.

Relationships are not the reasons why two hearts connect. This world is full of surprises and when two people are meant to be together, no matter what, life will twist and turn and bring them close. They looked at each other and nodded. Unsaid words are more meaningful at times and when her best friend asked her why she was marrying a man like Robert she said, "Well, who in today's world doesn't have a girlfriend? I know men who are into several relationships, and yet pretending to be bachelors in search of the next women. And there are women waiting for men; then why is it a scandal to marry a man who was once married and now divorced?" Maya felt that being in relationships and being married are the same thing with a little change in dealing with the family responsibilities. She blurred the days gone by and looked at Robert who wished for love and bonding in life like any human desires. He was someone who had been hurt and who made a mistake of accepting a marriage because of his parents' emotions. Maya would not let that be a reason to leave him and go.

She did not know what love was but felt a strange longing to be with Robert. At times he was lost and worried that their future might be on different tracks and he must let her go, but each time he had tears in his eyes. He loved Jenny, he would remember his wife, he would always know the pain that he has gone through and it would be difficult for him to leave his habits of smoking and drinking, yet there was something in Maya that made him feel complete. It could not be love since he had witnessed it before. But then what was it?

His family members were skeptical and they wondered if Maya is the right woman for their son. They warned him and asked him to wait this time, but Robert could sense a serene life ahead. A blissful life that would offer everything to him; he could not explain this feeling but he just knew that Maya was his better half. And he thought how he had been excited when he met Jenny, how he had been worried when he married his wife but after meeting Maya, he felt everything was just fine. The river has found its way to the sea and both of them agreed to be together without many words of commitment. The story of their lives has nothing extraordinary; it's a simple plot of falling in love like they did in the old times.

And Maya gave that letter to Robert on their wedding night. He smiled and kissed her forehead. They did not take vows and did not promise to be together forever; instead, they told each other something that astonished everyone present on their wedding day. They looked at each other, smiled and said together, "No matter what dear, we must grow old together!"

can love be loved with heart and soul,
can a woman be loved like none before ...

Love Vs Her

Written on a Terrace

'You need to show yourself at every opportunity because you most times no one can feel you!'

This is what she wrote to him in a letter, then put it in an envelope and posted it. She never shared the address with anyone even though she knew that everyone on earth was looking for this address. She can announce the discovery made on a winter evening when she was walking all alone in the hairpin curves of a hill station, and almost planning to leave that place. It was three months since she had come to that place and joined a school. She could have just visited the place and left in some days but something kept her there for a while. But after three months she became restless and wished to leave. And one day while walking down that hairpin bend, she witnessed her first déjà vu.

The man came and stood close to her when she was deciding to leave or return back. "It's a tough decision!" He said.

"I have not asked for your advice." She said, looking at him. He looked so familiar, someone whom she had known for a long time. "Did we meet before?"

"Yes, many times."

She was not sure. She kept looking at him and decided to end the conversation. But he continued.

"Look, I have come to your life and I shall keep coming each time you need me." He said with a smile.

She thought it was some prank and looked at him. His eyes were those of the lovers of her past, present and perhaps future. He was Love.

"You do not exist!" She uttered in astonishment.

"But I do…" He said looking into her soft brown eyes. "I do, I will always do.”

She ran up the mountain. The cold air was brushing against her cheeks and hairs but she did not stop. She was running away from that place since it gave birth to love in her heart. And each time she met a lover, she knew that her heart would break. It was not a ritual and she did try her best to adjust but nothing worked in the end.

And now Love himself was standing in front of her, she could not accept it and ran till her breath gave away and she sat on the road. Love came and sat beside her.

“How far can you run, woman? You can never leave me behind. The moment you were born, I was born in you.”

“Why in me and not in those men?” She asked in a hushed voice, panting for oxygen.

He laughed and said, “Of course I am in every heart, but is it my fault if you get attracted to other men and not someone your own match?”

“Match! I am thirty years old, and I still do not know who my match is…!” She laughed.

“Well, you are a woman. Born with your instinct, how can you not know who your match is?” He mocked.

She was ready to run again and this time she made up her mind not to stop at any cost. She ran as fast as she could. But after a while she needed to rest, since it is easy to walk down a mountain but climbing up needs real art and patience and she was lacking both at the moment. He came and sat beside her again, this time he looked angry.

“You cannot hide from me, woman. I love your very presence. You have to surrender!” He said.

“Never, I have not done that till now and I will not do that ever. Each time I have realised the man is not my kind or the man has no courage I have left him. I will keep doing the same…” She said in a loud voice.

He laughed. She was perplexed. She thought he would say something more dramatic, instead he kept laughing. She gathered her strength and got up. This time Love came and hugged her from behind.

"Leave me, leave me. You do this each time, you catch me unaware and I fall in love with the wrong person." She struggled to get free.

"There is no wrong person. You need to know your own match before falling in love." He said while holding her tight in his arms.

She tried her best but could not free herself. She gave up. "What do you want?"

"I want you to become my messenger in this place. This place has love in each corner but someone needs to show that to the people."

"Why me?" She wanted to know.

"Well, because I found only you one selfless woman. And I have witnessed that even when you do not find your match, you fall in love and spread goodwill. You do get disappointed after a while, and then leave in search of peace. It's a cycle for you."

"You are mocking my destiny. I hate you. Let me go!" She shouted. His fingers touched her lips and he pulled her face close to his. She stopped surprised. He kissed her, a long passionate kiss, which happened in the old world.

"You are my match dear. Until now I have not found a woman who can let go of men because they are not her match. I need you to help me to spread my emotions." He whispered in her ears and kissed them.

She could have fallen for his false words and let him touch her soul. But tears came to her eyes and even though she knew he was using her; she felt the need to spread emotions. She agreed. In the core of her heart, she hated him. They departed after a while and he gave her instructions. She looked at him for the last time and went up the mountain.

That day he had given his address with a warning that she could never visit him but if required could send him letters. She came back to the town, and soon began a non-profit organization. She taught the men, women and children how to love each other, while herself living in hope that one day Love would come back to her. Deep in her heart she hated him, and believed that he had hypnotized her and thereby she had agreed to serve humanity. What would she get in return? She never wrote him a letter. After a year of their meet, he started visiting her in sleep on every full moon night and made love to her. Each time she woke up and wondered whether it was a dream or did she fall in love with Love.

The town became a beautiful place and people from nearby lands came and settled there; everyone was happy and thanked her for showing them the value of emotions. She was peaceful except about one thing: the rule of not visiting Love. One day when she turned fifty, she wrote a letter and posted it. However, there was no emergency, rather she wanted to meet him. The letter was a love letter to Love. But she did not break the promise of visiting his home. She waited for a reply. She waited for days, and after a week she realized that Love was not visiting her dreams anymore. Two full moon nights passed away and Love did not come.

Yet she waited for the next full moon night. She looked out from her window and saw the serene night sky. The mountains around that place bloomed the beauty of solitude. Her eyes watched the stars and the moon and sketched another story. The next day people found that a rose tree had bloomed overnight in her garden, and she laid peacefully on her white bed, never to wake again.

will babies ever know that love, sex and birth
are three different dimensions ...

Drug Store

Written in Ooty

Love is neither blind nor selfish. It is a drug that pulls one out of a comfort zone and puts one in a new state. The heart pumps faster the moment the syringe enters this drug into the cells of a body that is unaware of the emotion, and then begins a story of disruption. The whole realm of mind dances in the unknown tune and the pulses wonder what could have suddenly gone wrong!

Amidst such a volcanic situation a relationship takes birth. The first time it breathes it does not cry, rather enjoys a demonic-laugh that no one can hear. They say in books that a relationship has its own fate to suffer the cycles of sorrows and happiness. No matter what, it has to go through all the phases and then it would sustain the battle of life and time. This is perhaps true or just someone's imagination; whatever may be the case, after it starts making decisions in a human's life, it becomes the sole caretaker till love takes over the role and a third person is born, a tiny human who can change the entire course of two adult human fates.

And such was the story of Henry and Daisy. Born in a town of South India both had been taught the values of highly conservative families. However, when Henry was sent to Bangalore for his further studies in Hotel Management, he snapped many rules. Definitely crossing the boundaries and giving birth to a relationship with a Hindu Tamil girl, Meenakshi. As her name suggests, Henry could not resist the drug of her eyes and fell for her in the first semester itself. Days were quite intoxicating since then and both travelled through time, imagining that the future would be waiting to welcome them.

But stories in real life cannot be like those on pages of a novel and so Meenakshi had to get married in her final year with a Hindu Tamil boy, arranged by her parents. All Henry could do was to drive his car three-thousand kilometers from Bangalore to Meenakshi's village to bid her goodbye and bury their relationship. The outcome was a realisation that he was very good with his car and could keep travelling to different places in search of solace and perhaps forget the death of his first relationship.

No one ever said that humans could give birth to a relationship only once, but Henry needed time after 'carrying to term' such a heavy load. And so, he left Bangalore and settled in Ooty, queen of hill stations in South India. A place that could give him silence and the hills; moreover, far Away from home and friends he decided to live a life in memory of his beloved. However soon he knew that he had to earn to survive on earth. Birth or death of a relationship cannot keep a human alive for long. He needs the basic requirements to live life. And so, Henry took up a job.

Soon his parents called him and urged him to get married. He could have said no, but his mother knew the ways to convince a son. Henry got married to Daisy. But this time a relationship was not born. The question was how will they stay together in such a situation?

To live together they needed the drug. Henry got himself busy with work, and Daisy had no clue. What was her story all this while? Well, she wrote in her diary on the first night; 'I cannot like him; he has stayed in Bangalore for so long. I am sure he had affairs. Why did he come back to marry me and waste my life...! I wish I could open my eyes tomorrow morning and this nightmare disappears...'

The morning came. And Daisy prepared the breakfast like she was always taught. All the values are taught to women so that on the first day of married life she could be confident in making her in-laws and husband happy. She was well trained and so she performed brilliantly. However, even though her in-laws smiled and praised her the whole day, she could notice how her husband looked lost. Oh, how much she hated him! She said her prayers that night and asked for mercy since she hated her own husband. But things would not fall into place unless the couple could take the drug soon. So, six months passed by and neither Henry nor Daisy smiled at each other. Looking at the situation the mother-in-law decided that the couple should live alone in Ooty while the other family members must go back to their native home. Daisy was quite unhappy. Henry had nothing to say.

Life took its own course and after three days of living together, finally they looked at each other since it was raining and Henry could not find the umbrella. Daisy knew her duties as a wife, and though each day she wanted to run away from her present home, yet she searched and found the umbrella and even smiled at him for the first time. Their eyes met, but the drug was missing. Either Henry's drug was over or Daisy never had it in her. The situation was quite complex; and in the blink of an eye four days passed by. On the eighth-day, Henry looked at Daisy and wondered why he was not feeling a rush of blood in his mind, like he did when he had met Meenakshi. A flash of memory jerked him in his past and present. He looked intensely at his wife. Daisy was quite good looking, there was a pleasant feeling when she was around and she was an excellent cook. What else can a man ask for?

'The drug and birth of a relationship; the pull and push and the magical world of sensations…' Henry dreamt of these words once long back when he had attended a relationship workshop with Meenakshi. An unacceptable decision for a boy who grew up in a town of South India, but at that time he had felt the urge to cultivate the drug in him to tie a knot around his girlfriend. He did wonder why he would need to do that since it has been always known that the woman should try to keep a man engrossed in her and in a relationship that they have given birth together. However, he decided that since he was attracted to his girlfriend, it did not matter who did what. But now it was a different story. It was his wife and that too someone he did not love. He could not decide whether he was attracted to her or not. But on the ninth-night he reached her side of the bed and pulled her close.

The morning came. And Daisy could not believe that it was already twelve o'clock and she was still drowsily lying on the bed. She looked around but Henry had already left for office. She smiled. What could have been the matter? Once when she was seventeen years old, she had felt the same intoxication. It was her cousin's birthday and five of them had hidden in a garage and drank cold beers. But this time it was something else, a sense of serenity. Only a drug could take a human to that level, in which nothing mattered anymore and the mind held onto the memory of the drug dealer.

In the evening Henry came back. To his surprise his house was decorated with Jasmine and tiny colourful lights. The table was laid with good food and there was a note from his wife: 'welcome back!' He nodded his head in utter astonishment and wondered, was it a good decision to marry a girl from his own town. He had no idea what her highest educational degree was. Moreover, he has seen and been around with women from the cities. Never did he think in his wildest dreams that he would marry a woman who would not know how to begin a conversation and now came a note which was hilarious. He quietly went to the bedroom and slept.

For a week Daisy tried to understand the reason why her husband walked around the house like a stranger. They had hardly communicated after that day. And she could not figure out his disposition even after so many months of their marriage. She had tried to ask him if anything was the matter but Henry kept saying that he was busy with his office work.

Four months passed by and the season changed to spring. The couple went to visit their homes. Henry decided that Daisy must live a few days with her parents. She wanted to protest but realised that women hardly had a voice when it came to their husbands' choice. Silently she agreed.

After a week when Daisy called Henry's mother to ask if her husband would come to take her home, the mother-in-law was surprised.

"But Henry went back to Ooty two days back, he said that he will pick you up on his way!"

"What?" Daisy whispered.

"Dear girl, did you fight with him?" the woman asked curiously.

Yes, Daisy wanted to scream. But she remained calm and said, "No, it's okay *amma*, I will call him…"

There is no point in wondering why Daisy had not called him earlier, and why did Henry leave without her.

Two months passed by. Henry wanted to call home and ask why Daisy did not try to contact him. But he thought that would give both his and her family members a chance to accuse him. So, he focussed more on his work.

Daisy's due date was three months away. She had taken that drug on that very first night and that had resulted in a revolution inside her. Many a times she had imagined an abortion but such is the birth of a relationship that it will not let a string get cut easily. And Daisy chose to suffer the cycles of loneliness, sorrows and expectations.

Henry's parents could not believe that their son could do such a thing, and when Daisy's parents announced that their daughter would be happy with a divorce, Henry's mother called her son.

In the evening Henry went to a park near his house. He wanted to sit alone for a while and ponder on what he had done and why. That night when he wanted to accept his wife, everything was perfect until Meenakshi sent a message: 'I am going to have a baby!' The meaning of his life altered. How can she be so happy? Did not they decide that they would create a future together and now when she would be a mother; it was not his child…

And the story could have ended here: Henry could have pretended to be happy while Daisy would have thought that her husband was interested in her. That's what happens in novels or short stories. Instead, the drug made his heart and mind selfish and he wanted Daisy to taste the drug too. If he was suffering then she must feel it, and he made love to her that night.

However, sometimes in life even from negativity comes out positive virtues, like the birth of a Lotus. And after one year, when Henry kissed Daisy, their baby giggled. Perhaps his little heart already knew that soon it would be his turn to take the drug. After all babies are manifestations of this universe, created to carry forward the legacy of the souls travelling on earth in human forms.

*tragedies are made out of anger, desperation
and greed of futile power ...*

Death Of Emily

Written in Ooty

Death of a close one always creates a vacuum in the depth of the hearts; it could be a human's or an animal's heart, and that happened when Emily died. The situation created an empty space in K. County and most of the residents took a long time to overcome the silence of her absence. The cows in the neighbourhood stopped chewing the grasses, the dogs did not bark for several days, the cats were not seen near the milk bowls and the birds silently gathered around Chirp's open cage. The door of that cage was always kept open since Emily said that her parrot knew manners.

In a small country like K. people knew each other by names and they all were aware about the magical things that little Emily did. She was nine years old, had black curly hair, ebony smooth skin, big dark brown eyes and a smile to offer anyone who needed compassion and love. The place of her birth was a cheerful one and the people lived like one big family. She was born to parents who were doctors and was the youngest of the three children in the Roseate family. She loved everything about life and cared for all those, whom she met. Her father was her favourite while she adored her mother. She grew up learning how to communicate with the nature around her and the birds, animals, trees became her friends. Emily's mind evolved at a very early age and made her different from the children of her own age. She read books on philosophy, psychology and travelogues with her own school syllabus, an interest and exposure that she got from her parents. But when it came to sports and playing with other playmates, Emily struggled to connect with them. She preferred to remain indoors and visit the library, helping her parents or the librarian Mr. Percy. Her siblings, Peter and Jenny accepted her as their sister but could not develop the same wavelength with her. However, Emily never felt left out, rather she got more involved in acquiring knowledge about the world around her and the universal ideas that connected humans.

Joan of Arc's story made Emily determined to eradicate false beliefs, superstitions and cruel intentions of greed. She wanted to keep her County free from negative influences and when she declared this in her speech on a particular festival morning, everyone clapped but laughed and called her naïve. She later asked her parents why the neighbours thought that her words were meaningless, to which her mother told her that it was her age and she was too young to change the world! Emily smiled and nodded. But that incident had made her more inclined to the ideas of upliftment and perspectives. Since then, she had started a club, in which each evening she met the members and discussed books, writers and visionaries. Soon the County' children had different things to explore and most began to question the ways the world around them worked. The parents noticed this change and, in some ways, they were happy that their children were sensitive to life and living. None were allowed to be rude and Emily made sure that the club members were kind, sensible and responsible.

But one family did not like what was happening in K. County. The guardian of that family was Mr. Roseatte's cousin sister Maria Sonnet. Her theory in life was to remember the past and either cherish or hold onto it. She could not accept that someone from her own family tree was exploring new ideas and executing them, not only alone but involving the whole neighbourhood. Soon in the County people freed their pet animals and those that got adapted to domestication or were unable to walk and fly after being in a cage for too long, they were kept like family members in the open ambience of their former owners' houses. Emily's parrot Chirp lived in an open cage. Her Aunt Maria never understood the importance of freeing the animals. But Emily knew that it was the first step to make her County a more liberal place to live in. wisdom is a dangerous form of freedom, something that begins with tiny steps and soon takes leaps beyond one's present imagination; and if not guarded well then, the myopic minds plan and begin to look for ways to destroy it. Emily was only nine years old and not adept enough to understand the games that some adults played when they were bored with their own lives.

Maria called a meeting; it was a Roseate-Sonnet family meeting. She wanted her cousin to understand the danger of changing minds in a society. Emily was playing with fire and if anyone felt attacked then their family would be criticised and tormented. Mr. Roseate laughed and said, "But Cousin Maria, Emily is a bright girl and she has a kind heart." Maria was not convinced and she stated that she could not let her own children be in danger of any sorts and she demanded to cut off the family ties. Everyone was silent. Then Emily stood and said, "I am a part of you as you are a part of me aunt Maria; we are individuals but with similar origins. And unless we exist together, this family will collapse and nothing new will occur." Everyone looked at her. Her parents smiled. And Mrs. Sonnet uttered words of astonishment, "But she is only nine years old!"

Her children Alex and Evan clapped their hands. They were two proud members of Emily's club. But even after such merits and presence of mind Emily had to die! And the death of Emily changed the entire story. On a dark cold night thousands of spiders from nowhere covered K. County. They blocked doors, windows, and all spaces that could be opened. Everyone in that place was sleeping and no one saw anything. The spiders crawled, reached everywhere and finally went up Emily's each strand of hairs. Not even one person in K. County was aware that Emily's subconscious mind was foretelling her near future; so, when she woke up from her sleep that night, she looked lost, confused and wished she knew the truth of the existence of the big black spiders. The next day she related her dream to her father, and then both of them checked the internet and books but they could only find that 'dreaming of spiders meant- one is feeling like an outsider in some situation and also it indicated a symbol of an overbearing feminine power in the dreamer's life...'

"However, father, spider was an ancient symbol of mystery, power and growth; and served as a reminder that our choices construct our lives," Emily said cheerfully. Dr. Roseate nodded. "I have decided to be a father..." But before she could continue, they heard loud thudding noise outside.

K. County had never known something called Religion. That morning when Emily and Mr. Roseate went out they saw a crowd outside their home, and a big car in the middle of them. The residents looked puzzled while among them Maria Sonnet came forward and welcomed the man in white suit in the car.

"Who is he?" Whispered Emily but before her father could reply, her aunt Maria introduced the words 'religion and its keepers'.

"Everyone let us welcome Mr. Robin, he is a scholar, preacher and researcher of the Theology." Maria announced proudly. "Our County needed someone like him!" She called the minister of the County close and asked him to present flowers to Mr. Robin. They smiled and looked straight at Emily.

Emily had never heard about the word religion from her elders before, and she asked inquisitively, "What is religion?"

Everyone looked at Mr. Robin and Aunt Maria. The man in the white suit laughed aloud like thunder. "Little Miss, I like curious beings. Religion is the miracle that humanity always needed to prosper. And I am the keeper of that reality, the rest is myth!"

Emily smiled and asked, "Mr. Robin in the books of wisdom I read, religion is a way of life, is that what you mean?"

"Shut up, you tiny…," Maria was furious.

"Relax Maria!" Said a calm toned voice. "No, I did not mean that Emily Roseate. I meant the values, old customs, rituals, orders and decrees. It is the reason why humans need to be in control and follow the paths of the chosen ones."

"You mean some kind of bondage!" Emily could not believe it.

"Oh, we do not need that, what do people say?" said doctor Roseate, "We are a free community that believe in freedom, peace and unity."

Everyone cheered.

"Goodbye everyone, we will meet soon in a different set up," said Mr. Robin zoomed away in his car with Maria Sonnet.

Emily held her father's left arm and said to all, "Only you can choose what is meant for you, remember the universe is alive and can hear you. Feel it dear ones!" That was the last day when Emily spoke. After that nothing remained the same. Within three days of the car's departure, a group of men came in search of the Roseate family. No one could identify them; they entered the house numbered 'three' in K. County and pulled Emily out. Her parents were attacked and kept inside the house. Her siblings stood on the terrace, horrified. They silently watched how their youngest sister was dragged mercilessly in the public.

No one till date knows who those men were; they had taken Emily and tied her to a nearest tree and proclaimed her to be a witch; someone capable of black magic and unfortunately the reason why the great Mr. Robin died. Everyone reacted and was surprised. They had forgotten about that man in the white suit. Suddenly Maria Sonnet came to that spot and gave details of how Mr. Robin had died two days earlier. It was a very confusing situation but those men declared 'death of Emily' to which the entire K. County rioted, even the animals and birds came to that place in angry gestures. The trees swayed and moved with force and a storm came from nowhere. Amidst such chaos, Emily's father was shot and he died on spot. Emily saw it all. She did not utter a word. She kept looking at the scenario, the people were confused and scared, Aunt Maria was laughing, her mother was crying, her siblings were scared, nature was violent, and her father's dead body.

She kept looking, dazed and lost in thoughts. She could neither speak nor cry. Her existence did not revolt that her father was killed; she did not move an inch. Someone had cut the rope which had been used to tie her to the tree, yet she did not react. The confusion in K. County passed away after an hour, when the sirens filled the place. The police came and sorted the situation, the officers took away doctor Roseatte's lifeless body, Aunt Maria went with them crying like a baby. Her mother kept sitting like a stone beside her dead father, while her siblings stood beside her.

Emily had died at that moment.

alive and breathing
silence and fighting
relations are confusing elements of life

we must endure, we must love
we must say we care
to our loved ones ...

Destiny Meets Me

Written Long Back

Her eyes told me that she has seen the same dreams, which had given me hope once. She was neither my reflection nor my friend. I looked at her for a while, and then delved into my own thoughts. The club was filled with cheerful laughter and happy conversations. What else can one expect in a nightclub where people come to exploit their emotions in order to forget themselves for a while!

A conversation with her could have given me a story. Life has given me one lesson: stories are very important to relate events. There is a link in everything; connections. And discovering a connection is a moment, which liberates us. It makes us feel that we are not alone. There is no solo struggle in this world; all are somehow attached with connected strings.

She looked at me; perhaps I imagined. But her intense eyes captured my attention. She looked confident yet there was restlessness in her eyes, as if they were searching for something in that crowded club. The club was built in the eighteenth century. But with the modern furniture, expressionist canvases and frenzied ambience, had a feel of chaos in the midst of a bygone era. Ambience has always been an important factor for thoughts to take shape. A thought could turn into an idea and then manifest into reality. This is a tested process.

A man came and took the empty seat beside her. He looked familiar to me. Sometimes we find faces from our past lurking at us from nowhere. It could have been my imagination but I noticed the birthmark on his right hand. He was my friend. Someone I met five years back and have known for three years. The last two years in between then and now have been a struggle to erase some memories. Is it ever possible to forget moments; is it wise to think that we can remove the unwanted thoughts from our subconscious mind and let new ideas takeover? A very positive way to put forward this idea is:

sometimes, something good needs to end to make room for something much better. It's like a hope that something better is waiting for us if we give up now and tread towards the next option.

Now I was more interested in her story. Where did her story with my friend begin? Was it working or was it about to end like mine? It's a curious fact how relations begin and end magically. Sudden meeting with someone creates a struggle in us to know more about that person. If we cannot comprehend that human, we are drawn more to him or her. It's difficult to understand why this episode is so common in our lives. But it continues like the Oedipus complex, until one day we believe we have met our soul mate. Our interest in cosmic powers makes us believe in the possibilities of uncertain realities and gives us new ideas to explore. Is a soul mate our need or our belief?

My friend, sitting across from me, was engrossed in some conversation. Did he notice me? Perhaps not; how strange at times we behave! We try to avoid people who were once close to our own hearts. At moments we cannot think of our world without certain relationships and each day during the moment of that 'closeness' our thoughts and feelings revolve around them. Psychology might have technical terms for the situation but in my process of thinking I could not explain that. For a while I wanted him to see me, and I plotted to call the barman loud enough for the entire night club to hear but as I was about to use my vocal cord Kabir took the girl's right hand and kissed it passionately.

My cell phone beeped at that crucial moment: 'Are you, their princess?' And instantly I wished I could vanish. I typed back:

A forest burning somewhere
the ashes are well hidden
only if you can come and
save a world from exploding

And then I kept my phone on silent mode. What's the need of distractions in the middle of a moment when contemplations are crawling around with vodka?

I could not see the ceiling. It was dark and the music was loud enough to make us deaf. A Saturday night could have been better spent with friends but sometimes we become loners and it's very difficult to explain the reasons. And not necessarily the reasons have to be grave and serious. Earlier that evening I had won the award of the youngest entrepreneur in the country and that made me feel I needed to be alone for a while. We hardly spend time with ourselves.

The couple went to the dance floor and I was mixing my drinks.

"Was that a good idea?" A man asked me as he came and shared my table.

"Definitely not! I cannot afford to share my table with another man," was my honest answer.

"I was talking about gifting Mr. Kabir Singh that beach house last year."

I looked carefully this time. It was my lawyer. I chuckled blankly. That beach house was almost forgotten. Of course, the gifts that we give our beloved are raindrops from the shower during a hot summer morning; they are never enough.

"What brought you here Mr. Alok?"

"I wanted to spend some time alone. My daughter got married yesterday."

"Brilliant!" I was overwhelmed.

"I saw him dancing with someone in this club. Did you notice him?"

"No. I have forgotten to notice things for a long time." The truth which is never true is that 'we forget the scars which life has given us. Also love stories are out of fashion in worlds of ambitions and money. And so, the lies about forgetting the past shine like the moon in the dark night sky. My fourth drink was a torture to my taste bud and I wished my consciousness could take over my subconscious thoughts and jealousies. Such emotions evolve in humans! The same flesh-and-bone structure can be both sweet and sour.

"Mr. Alok, do you believe in destiny?"

"Yes, and I know why you are asking me this question. We never met without legal reasons Ms. Radhika, but I know almost everything about you." Perhaps he did not understand my question. I looked at his glass of whiskey and ordered another bottle for him.

"I am sure you know that I am destiny's least favourite child."

He looked quizzically at me and after gulping whatever was left in his old glass, he took the replaced one in his hand. "What are you saying? Oh, humour... you are full of humour." And he started laughing. Was he mocking me? This is what liquors do; they break the barriers and bring out the original selves. But I was not a person to tolerate such comments from my lawyer or whoever.

"Maybe you should go home Mr. Alok," perhaps he did not hear me.

"You are an angel's daughter; they say at the office. You have reached such heights without support and whenever the stock market is vulnerable you are at your best."

I never analyzed my success. It had always been about what I lost in life. My parents had to go abroad without my grandmother and I revolted to stay back with her. My dream of becoming an engineer vanished when my father decided his daughter must get married. The man who was perfect for me, gave me roses with thorns and after three years of engagement he felt we were not compatible. And finally, I decided that I wanted to be alone and rich. Being rich would give me freedom since I noticed in the society how the women were given chances to bloom only to be crushed repeatedly.

"Ms. Radhika destiny has given you such experiences in life that have made you insightful and the seeker of truth. It shows in everything you do. Such poems you write!"

I scribbled on a tissue:

A land of my own
meanders in yours
and reaches a lost

desert full of cactus
yet I find my land
happy that I let it
explore

There were absolutely no reasons why I wrote that poem. I was not a writer and I never planned to publish a book. However, his words were making me think.

"You are a precious stone mined out of a coal mine."

"You are drunk and you need to go home." I hate sweet words without reasons. Somewhere I read that humans are strange at times and I am one of them.

"Ms. Radhika you are someone destiny meets every day but today I felt that you are not aware at all. Perhaps someday you will know." And spilling such words he rose to leave. So many times, in our lives we hear words that we already know deep inside but we deny to believe. Perhaps that makes us human. As Mr. Alok left, my attention was captured by an incident. Kabir was dragged by some barmen and his new love interest was shouting obscene words about him.

I was perhaps under the effect of my mixed drinks, and I texted my lawyer: 'Get my beach house back in a week.' It was time to leave that night club. It had already shown me what it was supposed to. My grandmother used to teach me that 'everything has a purpose' and I have learned to believe those words.

With the check I gave a piece of tissue paper to the barman:

Where will you find
a better 'you' in a world
of lost games?

Perhaps if you believe
in destiny then you
would look inside

to find the tricks and
rules to win those races

and train yourself for the
eagle's glide.

Some Words That Will Linger Forever ...

Soulmates

Written in Dreams

I cannot walk through the rain anymore. Or perhaps I can... I cannot say. It has been ages since I have felt those drops on my face. Do you ever feel magical when it drizzles and after a while your hairs write a different story?

I remember... I think I remember that day. The first time I realised it was raining. I am not sure if it was the first time. But right now, I see myself on the terrace of my old home.

The first shower after a long, humid summer. My feet are running in collected rainwater on the terrace. It was a game my mother used to play with my father. The water was never clean. But we loved those mornings and afternoons.

Not the nights. I was always afraid of thunderstorms. I still am. Perhaps I always will.

It is strange how we leave behind parts of our lives and go back to them at times. I miss my old home. I grew up in it.

And now I am another person. A traveller in a book of history.

Lost Opportunities

Written in Post Anger-Period

Sometimes we cannot see what we need to, yet there are times when we witness things that are not true. Such is the predicament of life, and in the midst of this we have to continue to live. The worst moments are when we hurt our own parents or loved ones by declaring how much we hate them.

Is it true? Do we hate them?

There are times we tell them to leave… leave us forever. And let us live in peace!

And one day suddenly emptiness engulfs us, and we hear the echo of our own voices.

They leave without words…

We remain to wonder what life is…

Voices call out again and again, yet only loneliness and fear oscillate in darkness, hoping that the light will bring back those souls.

But nothing can be grasped anymore. Only shadows and memories linger around.

Karma

Written in Thoughts

One day has to come when we will leave all our essences that have grown with us and turn to a new self. And this happens after a major change in life. Sometimes we all make mistakes and take our own calls but what about those moments when we sacrifice for the good of others. Karma still plays a role.

And then we float towards our own journeys but will anyone ever understand that sacrifice, perhaps not and even possible that we would be misunderstood and left alone. Such instances are not very rare. Amidst all these too people achieve their dreams and happiness.

It's difficult to understand the flow of life but perhaps nothing matters at the end or everything matters. It's up to us how we take life. But blessed are those who can create and bring something new around them. There must be people who admire, hate or love you or maybe just being with you because they are alone in this world for a while and are holding onto you to keep you alive.

Hardly matters. You must just leave all these behind and move forward. And be with those people only whom you want to be with. It's not at all selfishness, rather it's the best that you can do for yourself in your lifetime.

Love

Written in Clouds

Love is a strange dream that floats around us like tiny particles of our own essence. We love and we do not love. We find love and we lose love. We create love and we destroy love. But do we at all think for a while what is love...

Nothing, I would simply say it's nothing but a feeling that is born deep inside us the day we were born. The moment our tiny fingers touched Earth's atmosphere we felt love and then we cried, since we felt that this emotion will keep us alive till we tread on this planet.

Yet as we grow up the story changes and somehow love becomes an idea. We stretch it the ways we want, and the way people around us want and even make it a game, finally realising that it cannot be defined the ways we want. Rather it is always present in our core in the purest form. Have you ever tried the honey directly from the beehive? What you must have felt is a raw sense and taste. Yes, anything pure is wild and raw. So is love.

What we try is to tame it and make it our own kind. Not possible. The more we try the far it moves away from us. Let it be in its raw form. Feel it and live in it. It will grow around you. The simplest way to say this is, a cat loves you, a bird loves you and even a baby loves you without any connection or attachments. Love has its own flow; it has nothing to do with attachments or connections. It is you and it breathes with you.

Flashes of Some Words That Echo In The Darkness …

Another Me

a silhouette fading in walls

of streets

she walks towards her destiny

but it wasn't night yet, the

day denied to leave...

Warm wet eyes looked outside the metro this morning, I was going through a transitional moment. This is not new since there are moments when I pass through these short intervals in life. But today was not like before.

Somehow a feeling lingered in my core that I have to discipline myself more. Why would there be a wish to keep my head on a shoulder and cry till my heart fulfils its emotional needs?

I am not a pessimist or a loner, yet life surrounds me with moments like this. Something inside me burned today. A wish to break free from my own shadows and chains. Why can we not find solace within ourselves when we go through a crisis?

Yet I am a human and I deserve love; I want to walk the paths shown to me by my loved ones, living with others in harmony.

While the metro was churning hot this morning, my heart was spinning in that heat. Since my soulmate - *Amma* went to her own home I have become more carefree and a sudden desire to find roots again has evolved in me.

I have not looked for anyone before and now my eyes look for a companion, a confidante, someone who would listen to me and someone to whom I will listen. I did not understand this until I met a man who was on a similar journey like mine, but perhaps a little more sorted.

What bothered me more was that I wanted to talk to him. Even though in situations like this I have never crossed boundaries but this time I wanted to break free. It happened. My thought-clouds accumulated and before it could rain in a new pattern the window in today's metro flashed a *deja vu* and I reflected on the idea - why am I looking at one side of the mirror.

The people we try to hold on at moments, might not be able to walk with us long. There can be layers of reasons and we have to either figure them out or just let go. But what will remain with us is our own world. I could have cried there in that crowd of commuters but I let my tears turn into a rainbow and felt a million-minute inner jolts. And when the train stopped at my station, I smiled at the thought that now begins another journey of holding myself within me. In case I wish to be with someone, it would be for being with that person and not because I needed support.

Today

words shall stay behind when I am gone,

dreams might come true in another's life

stars will hide and the moon will remain

till the sun rises with a new hope for you…

We all go through pain and loss, the cycle of dreams and ashes. And yet we hide our own feelings from those we want to be with. Some have no idea how to take a relationship to the next level and when they think about their future with another human, they wonder if they will meet the right one.

This morning I went to visit a lady friend of mine, who was about to leave for a tour without her husband and before leaving she was cooking a week's meal for her husband. I was surprised but like a good guest I kept smiling. At the end of the cooking session, she said how difficult it is to be married and one should not consider such a situation. I was quite baffled since a month back she has told me how important it is to tie the knot.

I looked at her and all she gave me was a smile.

This world is full of such ironies and again I sit tonight to think what this life is all about. An age-old question that we all keep asking ourselves looking at those tiny bright stars spread across the dark night sky. No answer has ever been given. However, we keep waking up to new mornings to take our lives to different dimensions. And this cycle continues until a different pattern enters our lives. Yes, our lives have patterns like causal, sampling, analogy, planning and evidence. These patterns define the path that we take in life. For instance, an action causes a reaction in our lives: a surprise makes us happy, and karma gives us choices.

While noticing these patterns closely we understand that there are connections among humans.

Each night that we leave behind brings a bright tomorrow, and each tomorrow turns into a yesterday.

Today is the only moment that walks with us through these illusions of time and space.

Vibrations

a tiny hole in the roof,

he notices the sunlight;

the rains can wait in

clouds...

It was a *Sufi* song that took me to a trance three days back. Sometimes the songs become a bridge and our feet keep moving forward and backward. There are days when I go classical and days when I reach punk's shore.

But music is not the reason why I am scribbling now while sitting in a shared Uber. And thinking why that girl sitting beside me is not even looking at me once. I mean when two people travel, even if that is for a while, they do share some vibrations. And as soon as she got down after thirty minutes, the words struck me.

The words came floating in my mind, attraction and distraction. I looked out from the taxi's window; the blue and white light of Maa bridge took me to a parallel world. In life we meet many people and sometimes we get attracted to a few. They become our friends or lovers but there are moments when we make some people our distractions.

What exactly is the difference? A fine line between the two cases. A positive flow of energy enters the lives of people who are attracted to someone and in most cases the feelings get mutually transferred in these cases of attraction.

While escaping certain situations and memories at times we try to fill in the gaps with distractions. Whether this is a good idea or not, I cannot answer. But these relations or feelings are not reciprocated by the opposite person, since distraction does not work like magnets.

While reading a few pages of Gita, I realised that humans are endowed with more than one option in most choices they make in life. And this is perhaps the reason for confusions and pains in human minds. It is indeed very difficult to decide and choose what is right for us. But then what can be done?

Perhaps at moments when choices are difficult, we should focus on the fact that life is what we have. The rest are illusions and everything depends on how we perceive it.

Together Forever

union on earth is a moment

that lasts till dawn meets dusk;

and then it's a story of love…

In the same house there were two rooms: in one an old couple and in the other a young one. It could have been a beautiful story but the plot was a different one. The wife of the old man was dying while the young couple was getting married the next day.

The old man was sitting with his wife and praying for either her new life or her peace in death; he was confused and sad but he knew it was his duty to pray and stay strong beside his wife. It was after all a journey together of sixty-five years.

While in the other room of the apartment the young couple was planning, laughing and thinking about their lives together in the coming days. The young man knew his duty and he was prepared for a new life. Even though he was apprehensive about his decision of marriage. He was after all very young and could have chosen a dozen girlfriends more before a settlement, but his beloved was a woman of such charm and with a kind heart that he agreed to marry, lest she chooses another man. He trusted her but there were thoughts and fears.

In the other room of the apartment, the old man cried. He hid his tears and came to his sick wife smiling. They talked about old days. He talked. She nodded and remained silent most of the time. He looked at her lovingly. He loved her; they had met many years back in a village fair. And he knew that she was his life partner; and then there were so many complications before they could tie the knot. But throughout his life he had trusted her. Even now when she was on her death-bed he trusted her; he believed that either she would survive the difficult time and be with him or she would die and soon take him with her.

The young couple played music that night - of love and togetherness. They were unaware of the dying old woman since in cities these days no one knows who lives in the next apartment! They celebrated the last night of their singlehood...

And the old couple celebrated life together for the last time. They spent the last night together forever…

In the morning, the young couple left the apartment to reach the court for signing some papers of marriage registration.

In the morning, the old couple were silent and then an ambulance came and the man left the apartment with his dead wife for cremation and signing some papers of death certificate.

About the Author

Anindita Bose

Anindita Bose loves to nurture various disciplines of art. As an academician, she mentors people for English Language and Study Abroad Programs. Her poetry collections 'I Know the Truth of a Broken Mirror' published by Writers Workshop and 'illuminate darkness – the fireflies' published by Raa Publication are widely acclaimed. As an independent script-writer, she created a Bengali short film, Anubhobe (2020). Her poetry films got selected in Glass House Festival 2020. Co-founding Rhythm Divine Poets, a poetry group in Kolkata, has been a milestone in her life. She is the editor for EKL Review, and the Festival Manager for Chair Poetry Evenings, Kolkata's International Poetry Festival. She co-edited the short stories' book Dynami Zois [Life Force] published by Virasat Art Publication. Her experience of work extends to subtitling short films of vernacular languages. As a translator her credits are - Tales of Forest & Daily Cartoons About Kashmir translated for Institute of Social-Cultural Studies, Alexander's Hidden Treasure & Satan Is Awake translated for Biva Publication, My Daughter for Virasat Art Publication. Poems of Poets & Authors: Hindol Bhattacharjee, Rehan Koushik, Gourob Chakraborty, Abhimanyu Mahato, Arnab Saha, Jayati Roy.